T0198881

IMAGINED TALES

from

SOUTHEASTERN

NIGERIA

SIMON OTTENBERG

To order additional copies of this book, contact:
Xlibris
844-714-8691
www.Xlibris.com
Orders@Xlibris.com

ISBN: Softcover   978-1-6698-7310-5
            Hardcover   978-1-6698-7309-9
            EBook   978-1-6698-7308-2

Library of Congress Control Number: 2023906388

Print information available on the last page.

Rev. date: 04/06/2023

I thank Carol Ottenberg for a thoughtful reading of the text of this publication.

The front-page photograph, taken at Afikpo in 1990, includes five Afikpo elders and Simon Ottenberg. The Yellow wool cap indicates membeship in the most senior grade. The red caps mark those who are junior elders

I began writing these papers during the Spring of the pandemic of 2022, and I finished them in the Fall of the same year. All of them are partially based on actual events at Afkpo, an Igbo people, and all of them are also derived from my imagination. This form of writing is sometimes called historical fiction, a term whch is an oxymoron.

A heat wave actually occurred there. There were various reactions to it, and an oracle was consulted over it. A man from the countryside actually existed, who trained and worked in the city, and then returned to rejuvenate his rural village of birth. A boy illegally forced his was into the initiation of the vllage secret society.

All my life as an anthropologist I have tried to be factually accurate as best as I could. This is the first time that I have ever turned facts into fiction. I am surprised how much I enjoyed it.

Contents

❖

Farmland

It was March, the time to turn over the earth and to plant the crops. The rain would come, for the first thin white clouds were appearing over Ekere village. It was the time for the families to leave their village homes, to disperse to their small, separate farm settlements, and to begin the hard work of rice farming. After preparing the earth, it was time for men and women together to place the rice seedlings, one by one in lines, each plant separated by a regular distance from the next seedling, as if they were military units. It was also time for men to plant the yam seedlings and for women to plant vegetables.

It was at this time that Krakow appeared in Ekere village after eight years absence, living in a city, schooling, and working there. On his return, Krakow and his family were welcomed by his entire community as he was the first individual from the village who had studied in secondary school and had worked in a city. There was feasting, there was music by the village drummers and by a horn player. There was as girl's village dancing group, an exhibition of man's wrestling, a specialty of the village. There was much drinking of palm wine and native gin. Everyone was pleased to see how successful Krakow had been. He even wore different style shoes than they had ever seen before.

He soon met with the village's farmers, who hoped he could help them learn new farming ideas. A farmer, speaking in the local dialect, asked him about growing yams, the primary male crop. Krakow replied that he "did not study that and I cannot assist you. But I did learn English in school." None of the farmers spoke English. A woman asked him whether he could teach them how to grow better vegetables. Krakow replied that "He never learned about growing vegetables but that I has studied Shakespeare in school." " A woman asked him "What did Shakespeare grow?" No, no," he replied, "it was a play." The farmers grew quiet, not understanding what a play was. Eager to show his knowledge, Krakow said, "I learned all abut the kings of England." "Were the kings' farmers? "No, but farmers worked for them" "Did they grow yams? " No, it was too cold." A farmer quered him, "We have heard that there are better forms of rice then we grow here. Tell us about that." "You should consult the Agriculture Department." But I learned about the British Empire in school, and I can tell you many stories about it." The farmers gradually ceased asking questions and dispersed, disappointed in learning nothing about farming from this educated man. They began to ignore him.

Krakow had come to reside in Ekere at the end of the major dry season's activities—the weddings, the initiation into the male village secret society, the Yam Festival, the memorial services for the deceased,the title taking, the setting of farmland ownership disputes before farming began, and other major events. It was a time of considerable socializing.

When it ended almost everyone turned to independent family living on the farms for some five months, at least they did so about 1910, when this story took. place

Krakow father was responsible for the allocation of the family's farmland. The scattered farm plots each had a name that distingished it: Kola Nut. Raccoon, Eggplant, Thorn Bush, Crickets.The family members gathered at a designated place where the father told everyone where he or she would farm for a year. The general rule was that you farmed the same land every year it was available within a system of land rotation.

Adjustments were made for old age, deaths marriages, ad growining chidren. During Krakow's long absence one of his prized land section, Bananas, had been farmed four times by Inoka, a younger brother. He refused to give it up for the new farm season as custom usually demanded. A serious dispute broke out between the two brothers over the land. Krakow noted that he had farmed the land before he left for the city. He stated "I have returned to live in the village and this farmland is mine to farm. It is not the property of my younger brother." But his father, who could not believe that after eight years in the city that he really wanted to farm, said that the younger brother had farmed it four times in rotation and that the Krakow no longer had a claim to it. This family head allocated a much less desirable plot of land to the older brother called Pebbles. The older brother protested. "Even though I have been away for eight years I know our people's customs. Age conquers everything else. I am the older brother. I am entitled to take the land back." He attempted to farm Bananas but his father called in relatives, and they threw him off it.

Distraught, the older brother took his complaint to the village head, who was living on his own farm village some distance from his home. He refused to support the older brother's claim, saying, "You were away for eight years and not farming with the family. Go farm where you have been living for eight years. Or, farm the land allocated to you to show that you are still a farmer. If you do well. Your father will give you better land to farm next year.

But Krakow had decided to stay. No one could understand that after eight years living in a city and going to school that he wanted to return to village life. He told himself he did not know why, but it was quiet life. He wanted athe quiet life. City life was not happy life for him. He had missed his relatives and friends in his village.

Krakow did not understand what was happening to him. He complained about his farmland allocation to the village chief, who said to him, that "Your land allocation has been decided correctly at the family level, even though it violates the local principles of age priority. If you stay and live as a villager your age rights will be restored in time."

Krakow realized that he was no longer a member of the village and he quietly left for the city, where he obtained a job as a colonial government clerk. His wife and their children were pleased to return to the city. She did little farming at Ekere. She had vegetables sent from her favorite store in the city Their children were excited at first to be in a rural area, but they soon found little to do there. Although they often objected to schooling in the city, the country school did not stimulate them, and the dialect of the language was strange to their ears.

When villagers, especially fathers, saw that Krakow's father, a respected village member, had not followed the customary age rule in the case of his eldest son, and nothing terrible had happened to him, other village fathers began breaking customary rules. Then young adults, seeing that their fathers were now not following the rules, began breaking them themselves and leaving for the city. Within a few years there only remained a few miiddle- age farmers, and old and ill people in the village, who did little farming. The village was one of many in the region without a tradition of hired labor, and it was many years before the exstence of migant labor in Ekere vllage.

The Year of the Vegetables

❖

It had not rained for a long, long time. Dust settled in the children's eyes. There was constant crying. A strong hot wind blew into Ameta village in Nigeria's southeast. This was in the in early 1900s, when the British had recently gained military control of the area but were not yet in administrative authority.

The yam tubers were barely growing in the earth's dryness. They shriveled in the ground. The usual time of the annual Yam Festival was approaching when the new season's yams were first allowed to be harvested and consumed. But the yam tubers were small, dying in the dry soil. Yams, the basic village food, in a normal growing year were as heavy as eight pounds each, and up to four feet long. Men took pride in the only food they grew, a symbol of maleness, the penis of nurture. But this year the yams were very stunted. It was the heat of discontent. People grew irritable with one another.

The women's vegetables were not doing any better. Their greens were wilting. The remnants of the year's vegetables were fast disappearing. Goats, sheep, and chickens lay listless, thin and thirsty. The village stream flowed like pee.

The village elders sacrificed chickens, eggs, bits of cloth soaked in medicines, at their personal and group shrines again and again. They consulted diviners and herbalists. No rain came. The heat prevailed.

In muted tones the young men criticized their elders, the village leaders. They rarely did so outwardly. They believed that their seniors had lost their spiritual power. How could the village hold its annual dry season festivals without food-- the title taking, the marriages, the initiations of boys and girls, the wrestling contests and the memorials to the dead?

Nnachi the Weatherman lived at the edge of the village, and was believed to cause rain, lightning, and to bring good weather. Oso, the Yam Priest, lived in another village. He not only controlled the growth of yams but also set the time of the Yam Festival. Both priesthoods were inherited positions, father to first son, and they and their families were independent of the village authority of the elders who ruled Ameta. These two priests were aloof to everybody, though with their families they visited the local market.

As the village elders were upset, they met. Siaka complained "that in all my years I have never met a situation such as today's."

Another elder grumbled : "It is hopeless, A bad year. We have several times consulted diviners and herbalists and carried out their suggested sacrifices without results. What can we do?" Then Chukwu, an elder, quieted the gathering. "Eguni! Eguni!" he greeted them.

"By tradition we do not go to the Weatherman. He has his own ways, his own shrines. But now we must act. There is no rain. We need to smash this serious matter."

Chukwu chose five elders and approached Nnachi the Weatherman. They were surprised at how welcoming he was as they sat on dried mud benches covered with animal skins, with native clothes hanging on the walls and a house monkey jumping in excitement at the rare presence of visitors. After an initial joint prayer to the village high god, they chewed kola nuts together, a traditional sign of peaceful relationships, carefully holding the kola in the right hand. To touch kola with the left was an abomination, for it was the toilet hand.

Chukwu, was impatient. "Why the heat, why the poor crops, and why do our streams piddle like pee?" Nnachi gently replied: "I am pleased to have you here. My spirits foretold your coming." Chukwu replied: "I am pleased to be here and not pleased to be here. We ask you why the heat and no rain? The villagers are restless." Without revealing his magical methods, Nnachi indicated that a spirit that he was not yet able to control was blocking his work. Chukwu and the other visitors were surprised, for they had believed that he had more power. "But we cannot wait," Chukwu intoned. "We need your immediate help." Nnachi laughed. "The weather is slow business. You cannot hurry it. I will continue my efforts." The visitors left without any resolution.

Some villagers thought the Weatherman was old and had become spiritually useless. Others thought that Nnachi had personal reasons for keeping back the rain, although he had not asked for anything from the village. Still others had always been skeptical of his powers.

Then some elders considered consulting a famous oracle, Ochii, controlled by people speaking the same tongue as those in their village. This involved a an eight-day foot journey, and it was very expensive. Also, they had heard that some of those who went there never returned, disappearing into slavery, or killed by the oracle. But two middle-aged former warriors agreed to go and Chukwu, always an enthusiast of the spirit world, agreed lead them. Chukwu's village men in favor of the endeavor pooled their cowrie-shell money, for coins were not yet introduced into their village. Chukwu's third and youngest wife agreed to cook for them. An agent of the oracle living in the village agreed, for a fee, to lead them. Shortly after starting they became aware that groups from other villages with their own oracle agents had joined them. They realized that the oracle business was big business.

After an arduous trip, for Ameta's villagers never travelled far from home, they encamped at the oracle's village, to find other groups, sometimes speaking different tongues, also waiting to consult the oracle. About the weather, land ownership, inheritance, poison accusations and even murder charges. They waited four days. Their agent insisted on one more payment to ensure their safety before the oracle. Then he led the three men into a deep, wet, dark, gorge. They shivered upon hearing strange rumbling sounds and voices. Then a loud, echoing male voice asked them why they had come Chukwu explained about the heat and the dried-up crops, complaints the oracle must have heard before. There was a long moment of silence. Then the voice asked: "Have you made an offering at all your village shrines?" "Yes, yes, Many times," Chukwu shouted into the darkness, "but the heat is still with us."" Have you sacrificed to the spirits of Ilefe and Umusu?" "No, no, don't know them," Chukwu responded. The voice went on: "Shrines are shrines, but some spirits are more powerful than others. The world of spirits is not as you know it. Eggs are eggs but some are rotten." There was quiet, and then there was another terrifying rumbling. Their agent said it was time to go.

They started home the next day, arguing over the meanings of the oracle's pronouncements. For a fee, the agent agreed to help them establish and care for the two shrines.

On their return Chukwu called together the entire village and informed them of the oracle's sayings. He indicated, to the farming people, how expensive the trip had been and the creation of the two shrines. both with the help of their agent. The villagers were surprised at this costly venture and expanded on various interpretations. However, the elders and other villagers created the shrines, and prayed at them as the oracle had suggested. They waited and waited. Nothing happened, the heat was still there. The agent could not say why. He suggested another trip to the oracle, but even Chukwu, began to wonder about the nature of the oracle. They would not consult it again. Those who had opposed the trip and the shrines felt vindicated.

The days dragged on. One day, the village men who were at the age that they would have been warriors in the past, gathered with their leader Suku. They must do something about the weather. With clubs and machetes, they destroyed the Weatherman's home, but did not touch his shrines, whose spirits they feared. He and his family, unharmed, took refuge in a nearby village. This solved nothing, although it gave the attackers pleasure. Weatherman became ordinary man, only using his name, Nnachi and his shrines were rotting. "What can I do away from my shrines?" he asked.

The village elders ordered those who had destroyed his home to rebuild it. They reluctantly did so. He and his family returned to their new dwelling, although some villagers warned: "Do not come back unless it rains." They claimed he was too old for his work, but he rejected it, "I inherited this work. By tradition it is mine until I die. I will not retire."

Eight days after their return the wetness began, the rains lasting for many days, tu/rning dust into mud. It was too late for the yams to grow, and the Yam Priest delayed the Yam Festival for a year. But the vegetables did grow and everyone lived off of vegetables. For many years the citizens of Ameta wondered what had brought the rains. Was it a delayed response to the oracle's two shrines, or the Weatherman's efforts? But they were pleased since the rains had come. The time was remembered as the Year of the Vegetables.

The Swearing

❖

Eleke was accused of stealing a gun from Kalale in Deke, the village in which they both lived, but in different compounds. Eleke denied taking it, saying that it was Kalale's fault, as he did not care for his gun, allowing someone to steal it.

The incident occurred in the early 1900s, when the British were just beginning to take control of the twenty-seven villages called Ameke in southeastern Nigeria. They had introduced a standard rifle into Nigeria, and both Eleke and Kalale would have the same make.

A gun was a valuable and prized object where these two lived. Africans needed a special permit from the colonial government to own one. A hunter made a good living selling wild animal meat, wherever he was. This food was essential at manyl major African feasts, and hunters were essential for wild meat. It was still a time of many of these creatures. Later colonization would make them very scarce.

Eleke was known as a hunter, and he did not deny that he had a gun of the same brand as Kalale. Their families had been rivals for a number of generations, mostly over farmland holdings. The villagers shrugged their collective shoulders at Kalale's compliant, saying "What's new?

The two hunters took their dispute to the village elders. It skillfully debated as the two hunters presented their viewpoints. Their families had been at odds for many generations.

Kalale took the case to the higher council at Ameke of the twenty-seven related villages. It. Reluctant to make a decision with scant evidence, they asked Eleke to "swear juju," that is to swear his innocence before a special spirit shrine for all of these villages. Called Erape It judged the truth of what was claimed before It. If you swore your innocence and nothing bad happened to you in a year you had not lied to it. If you lied to it something serous would occur to you, such as crop failure, a major illness or the spirit could kill you, or you had an accident, or something tragic happened to your family.

Anxiety over swearing innocence, while actually lying, made you confess having lied to the shrine spirit. Erape. If any of these, or a similar fate occurred within a year of swearing, you were considered guilty and you were fined by the council.

If nothing happened to you, you held a victory celebration, which in a sense mocked the accuser. But many who were guilty of something but swore their innocence applied medicines or salves, or visited a diviner, to attempt to avoid the curse of this powerful spirit.

Eleke did not see why he had to take the oath. " I have d wrong," he declared before the council. "It is my accuser who should be made to take the oath, not I." But the council insisted.

Eleke, in front of witnesses, reluctantly swore his innocence before a clay pot containing earth, many broken eggshells and bird feathers, located at the edge of one of the Makame villages.

He did nothing further concerning the swear for a few months, feeling confident of his position, and since nothing unusual happened to him. But Eleke became aware that Kalale might be using medicines that would make Eleke confess, whether he had lied or not, He was right. He found out that Kalale had obtained a powerful medicine to make Eleke confess, whether he was guilty nor not.

Eleke was certain that Kalale would use medicines to try to make him confess. Although Eleke felt he was innocent, he wondered whether he should protect himself. He consulted another diviner. He was sympathetic, recommending that Eleke always carry the dried leaves of a certain plant wherever he left his compound during the remaining year of the swear. Eleke found the leaves in a bush near his village and followed the diviner's recommendation. This made him confident that he would win the dispute

Bur after nine months he thought that he was beginning to become ill. He consulted a well-known herbalist who gave hm paste to rub on his left arm to protect himself. The symptoms of illness disappeared.

Eleke finished the year with a large family celebration. The council fined Kalale for accusation. He never located his gun. However, he was able to procure another one at some expense. He scratched special markings on it, in the event that this problem arose again. Eleke did the same.

Kalale was still convinced that Eleke had stolen his gun and had somehow fooled the spirit of the shrine. The hostility between the two families continued.

The Boy

❖

It was the time of year, after the harvest season. for stick fighting and the initiation of boys into the village men's secret society, which would follow on the next day. Ten fathers had paid the necessary dues for both events. Only Ikwuma was left behind. His father was dead, and his guardian, Uncle Alono had again put off paying the expenses, as he had done so in past years. Known as "Stingy Man" in his village, he was reluctant to pay, for as he explained, "There is no money in the boy." Ikwuma's inheritance had been assigned to relatives. The nephew, Ikwuma, was discouraged. He did not believe that his uncle would ever pay to put him through the rites,

Neglected by his relatives after his mother also passed away, Ikwuma wandered about, refusing to take part in boys' activities. He was a loner, begging food at times. He was caught stealing food again and again and beaten for it. A rascal boy.

This year he was determined to do the two rites. Although no one had paid for him he simply sat in the arena with the ten boy imnitiates whose parents, or other relatives, had paid for the privilege of watching stick fighting all day, and for the initiation beginning the following day.

These other boys shunned and beat him, knowing he had not paid, but he remained seated. The stick fighting leaders told him to leave. He refused, saying, "I have the right to be here." His uncle was not to be found. Finally, a wealthy distant relative, Ekechee, who knew of Alono's character and financial ways, paid for both Ikwuma's events, the stick fighting and the initiation. But only if Ikwuma worked for him on his farms after the initiation. Ikwuma, eager to be involved, agreed and remained seated. The initiates ignored and beat him. He sat alone. They regarded him as an interloper.

To frighten the eleven seated boys the leaders in the stick fighting told them that they would be stick fighting the next day when they were initiated.

The boys, whether frightened at this information or not, remained seated and quiet.

Ikwuma noted that no females were present. "This must be a day to try men," he thought. He observed the day's event very well, since living as a loner had taught him to observe everything very carefully. He saw that there was another audience, men middle aged to elders. They shouted encouragement to their favorites and gave forth with hostile words to those they disliked. "They must have been stick fighters when they were younger," Ikwuma thought.

He could see that the referees, wearing raffia hats and all about the same young adult age, were lining up pairs to fight by size and height, two fighters at a time. They saw that several pairs fought at the same time, starting with the youngest and going to the oldest, up to middle age. The contestants stayed in the ring all day, except for briefly leaving for a drink, Ikwuma noted, Maybe palm wine or native gin, as they became increasingly excited. The contestants wore only a waist cloth and he gathered from the action of referees that a fighter shouldonly aim at the body, and not the face, head, or legs. There were many cuts and some bleeding, but a fighter who paid attention to them was considered to be weak.

Ikwuma observed that a pair of fighters faced each other, and in turn beat one another. He had the impression that to cry out in pain or to turn away from the hitting was a sign of male weakness.

Ikwuma knew that in village wrestling matches there was music, and here there was none. He thought that in stick fighting the players absorbed such a high level of energy and excitement that music was not necessary. Wrestling was open for all to view, The referees were senior in age, and that there were intervillage matches, but none were occurring here. This was a different event.

By early afternoon, Ikwuma noticed fighters moving away from the arranged matches and challenging and fighting whoever they wished. There was a total loss of control by the referees and a fight for the rest of the afternoon, chaos, an exuberance of body and mind, which Ikwuma wanted to join in. But, along with the other boys, Ikwuma refrained from any public action, remaining as a member of the silent audience of boys. This was in contrast to the village seniors sitting next to the boys, excited by the action and the joyful, if painful, sense of the human body. A jolly, happy sense.

The referees began to lose control of the situation. One of them even joining in the stick fighting. Fr a few hours anyone challenged anyone to a fight. Some fighters declined, but were in danger of being called weak. Whipping lashes were occurring more frequently and these was increasing shouting from the participants. Ikwuma noted that the fighters were more and more breaking away from the arranged matches, the young referees having lost control. different sort of event, he muse. He wanted to join in the fighting, but since the ten boys remained seated and silent of making any public comment, Ikwuma also refrained from his egocentric, individualistic energy of recent years in his v1llage. He had to exhibit control as he was no longer wandering around his village, and as he looked forward to going through the initiation.

The fighting ended in the late afternoon. Ikwuma was sure that the women in the compounds knew what had been going on when the fighters returned.

Ikwuma and the other boys remained all night in then arena. Food prepared by their mothers was sent to them, but no food came for Ikwuma. Two initiating boys, who knew the eccentricities of his uncle, shared their meals with a grateful Ikwuma. The isolation of the ten boys from Ikwuma was breaking down.

We will not describe Ikwuma's experiences in the initiation, except to say that he did not rebel against any part of it. He was successful.

Afterwards he worked for Ekechee, who became like a father to him, for example, paying for his first title ceremonies, as a father should. Ikwuma became a good farmer and grew to be a leader in his village and a stout defender ofi the secret society.

Over time, he became one of its respected leaders, and a community leader. He had left behind his rascal image.

The Sculptor

❖

Uku sat alone on an undecorated round wooden stool that he had created when he first began to sculpt. Its lines were clear and its surface smooth. Other carvers in other villages than Ndzure fancified their sitting stools. To sit on the ground while sculpting would be an offense to the earth spirit *Ale*. Uku sacrificed to it before cutting trees for their wood, in order that this powerful earth spirit did not cause him to cut himself or to create poor work. Uku was the only person who ever sat on his stool, and he carefully wrapped it in cloth at the end of each day, `

Uku sculpted in a small sacred clearing in a forest near his home village; he was the only sculptor there. There were villages that had no sculptors, and several settlements had two. While the craft was inherited, it was also open to others; it was not a caste. Only males who were members of the village secret society were allowed to watch Uku sculpt, but this rarely occurred. and Uku did not object to the absence of others while he worked.

Uku thought his wives knew about his mask carving work from his mysterious absences from their village. They may have discussed it amongst themselves and with other women, but they never talked about it with Uku or other men. In that way the secrecy of the men's society was maintained. The wives had watched their sons' initiations from the outside and had gathered a good deal of information from watching the secret society's masquerades, all of which they shared only with females. They had loaned pieces of their clothing to a husband or brothers for their masquerade dress without more than minimum words being said, for some masqueraders represented women. From their sons' initiation into the secret society, they had gleaned information, which women secretly shared with other women, so there were really two secret societies, one for each gender, one highly organized and one quite informal.

Uku remembered a case where a woman had revealed her knowledge of the village male secret society to men. She was forced to carry out a small purification sacrifice at the men's secret society shrine, the only time she would ever be in the society's physical boundaries. This was a frightening experience for her, with the shrine priest and her husband both there. Her husband paid for the sacrifice, for he was considered responsible for her behavior as all husbands were for their wives. In addition, he was heavily fined by the secret society leaders for not restraining his wife from talk. He paid the society in English pounds, Nigerian currency not yet being available in his sector of Nigeria in 1910. While the women's spiritual sacrifice was small in cost, it was probably effective emotionally for it was unusual treatment for a woman and religious in nature. Her husband's payment was secular, as if in a court. There was no mechanism of appeal to the village elders, who ruled the community, or to the village head. In this case, the secret society was autonomous from external pressure.

There is no record of what the husband said to this wife or whether he whipped her or punished her in other ways.

Uku sometimes wondered how many women knew that he was a sculptor and how readily was this knowledge spread. But it really did not matter; he did not sculpt for women, nor reveal to his three wives what he dd, He also was not a creative innovator. He carved the usual style mask used in the masquerades, and for boys' initiations and he made them very well, always on personal demand, for the masks were privately owned, although stored in the dark interior of the men's village rest house located at one side of the open village center. Since childhood he had felt comfortable with his people's secrecy rules and had always followed them.

But now Scottish missionaries who had been in the region for some years opened a primary school in his village, and the colonial government insisted that all children, regardless of age, had to attend.

Uku had nine children by his three wives, and he had to pay school fees for all of them. In hindsight, he would not have taken so many wives, for schooling expenses altered an affluent man into a poor man. He saw that the older children would have less time to help him and his wife with the farming, and he learned that the missionaries would like to eliminate the secret society and the delicately crafted ties of secrecy between men and women, although it had not as yet threatened the ending of masquerading and the creation of masks.

Uku felt that he was part of the secret society and that if he were to make masks for anyone not a part of it, that would be in violation of his trust in the society. But then he discovered that secret society members were selling their masks to outsiders of the secret society, even to stranger women.

He realized that the delicate balance of gender relationships of men and women had changed. Masquerades, which had served to criticize poor behavior, formally did so to assist in maintaining the rules of the society, but now they were only for entertainment.

Even his wives seemed to have changed. Before, when they sold vegetables at the market, they gave him the money and he gave them back a small portion to spend as they wished. Now they kept the money for themselves and give him a small amount to spend.

Uku could not control the changes. Everything was out of balance. He felt that his world had changed.

Even his wives seemed to have changed. Before, when they sold vegetables at the market, they gave him the money and he gave them back a portion to spend as they wished. Now they held the money for themselves and give him a small amount to spend.

Uku could not control the changes. Everything was out of balance. He felt that his world had changed. He would have too adjust to it.

He inquired of carvers in neighboring villages and discovered that both masks used in their secret society and new ones were being sold to strangers. Uku was shocked, particularly over the sale of masks used in masquerades, which when not in use were stored in the men's sacred rest house at the village center, for to Uku and others they were sacred objects. Though clothing that men wore at masquerades were not, dress even being borrowed by a masker from a wife or a sister.

Uku, the only carver in his village, who was a member of the inner circle in its secret society, went to consult its priest, diviner, and four senior members. He told them that he had requests to sell secret society masks and that carvers in neighboring villages were selling new society masks and even their society members were selling masks that had been used in their masquerades.

Uku offered a compromise. As the only carver in the village any masks that he made for the village secret society would not be sold. Any mask he made that was used by the secret society should not be sold. Any masks that he made to look like society mask which were never used in the society he was free to sell, but only secretly to a male rand no female should see it until the mask was out of Afikpo. The assembled group reluctantly agreed to the plan and that it would permanently solve the matter. Why did strangers want to purchase Afikpo masks? Did they have secret societies?

Uku saw this as a way to protect the secret society and still gain funds for school fees and other purposes. He was aware that his way of life was rapidly changing and that this might only be a temporary solution.

The forces of change created a delicate new balance, which would not necessarily last for long, requiring yet further changes in the village carving rules and the use of masks.

Printed in the United States
by Baker & Taylor Publisher Services